BLACK PANTHER
ADVENTURES

BLACK PANTHER
ADVENTURES

Marvel Adventures Fantastic Four #10
Writer **JEFF PARKER**
Penciler **MANUEL GARCIA**
Inker **SCOTT KOBLISH**
Colorist **SOTOCOLOR'S ANDREW CROSSLEY**
Letterer **DAVE SHARPE**
Cover Art **CARLO PAGULAYAN & CHRIS SOTOMAYOR**
Assistant Editor **NATHAN COSBY**
Editor **MARK PANICCIA**
Consulting Editor **MACKENZIE CADENHEAD**

Marvel Adventures The Avengers #22
Writer **MARC SUMERAK**
Penciler **IG GUARA**
Inker **JAY LEISTEN**
Colorist **ULISES ARREOLA**
Letterer **DAVE SHARPE**
Cover Art **LEONARD KIRK & VAL STAPLES**
Assistant Editor **NATHAN COSBY**
Editor **MARK PANICCIA**

Avengers: Earth's Mightiest Heroes #1
Writer **CHRISTOPHER YOST**
Artist **SCOTT WEGENER**
Colorist **JEAN-FRANÇOIS BEAULIEU**
Letterer **DAVE SHARPE**
Cover Art **SCOTT WEGENER & JEAN-FRANÇOIS BEAULIEU**
Assistant Editor **MICHAEL HORWITZ**
Editor **NATHAN COSBY**

Marvel Universe Avengers Earth's Mightiest Heroes #8
Writer **ELLIOTT KALAN**
Penciler **CHRISTOPHER JONES**
Inker **POND SCUM**
Colorist **SOTOCOLOR**
Letterer **VC'S CLAYTON COWLES**
Cover Art **KHOI PHAM & EDGAR DELGADO**
Editor **TOM BRENNAN**
Senior Editor **STEPHEN WACKER**

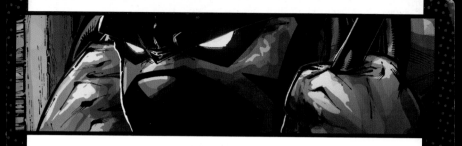

Avengers #52
Writer **ROY THOMAS**
Penciler **JOHN BUSCEMA**
Inker **VINCE COLLETTA**
Letterer **SAM ROSEN**
Editor **STAN LEE**

Avengers #62
Writer **ROY THOMAS**
Penciler **JOHN BUSCEMA**
Inker **GEORGE KLEIN**
Letterer **ART SIMEK**
Editor **STAN LEE**

Black Panther created by Stan Lee & Jack Kirby

Collection Editor **JENNIFER GRÜNWALD**
Assistant Editor **CAITLIN O'CONNELL**
Associate Managing Editor **KATERI WOODY**
Editor, Special Projects **MARK D. BEAZLEY**
VP Production & Special Projects **JEFF YOUNGQUIST**
SVP Print, Sales & Marketing **DAVID GABRIEL**

Editor In Chief **C.B. CEBULSKI**
Chief Creative Officer **JOE QUESADA**
President **DAN BUCKLEY**
Executive Producer **ALAN FINE**

BLACK PANTHER ADVENTURES. Contains material originally published in magazine form as MARVEL ADVENTURES FANTASTIC FOUR #10, MARVEL ADVENTURES THE AVENGERS #22, AVENGERS #52 and #62, AVENGERS: EARTH'S MIGHTIEST HEROES #1, and MARVEL UNIVERSE AVENGERS: EARTH'S MIGHTIEST HEROES #8. Second printing 2018. ISBN 978-1-302-91034-1. Published by MARVEL WORLDWIDE, INC., a subsidiary of MARVEL ENTERTAINMENT, LLC. OFFICE OF PUBLICATION: 135 West 50th Street, New York, NY 10020. Copyright © 2018 MARVEL No similarity between any of the names, characters, persons, and/or institutions in this magazine with those of any living or dead person or institution is intended, and any such similarity which may exist is purely coincidental. **Printed in the U.S.A.** DAN BUCKLEY, President, Marvel Entertainment; JOHN NEE, Publisher; JOE QUESADA, Chief Creative Officer; TOM BREVOORT, SVP of Publishing; DAVID BOGART, SVP of Business Affairs & Operations, Publishing & Partnership; DAVID GABRIEL, SVP of Sales & Marketing, Publishing; JEFF YOUNGQUIST, VP of Production & Special Projects; DAN CARR, Executive Director of Publishing Technology; ALEX MORALES, Director of Publishing Operations; SUSAN CRESPI, Production Manager; STAN LEE, Chairman Emeritus. For information regarding advertising in Marvel Comics or on Marvel.com, please contact Vit DeBellis, Custom Solutions & Integrated Advertising Manager, at vdebellis@marvel.com. For Marvel subscription inquiries, please call 888-511-5480. **Manufactured between 3/14/2018 and 3/26/2018 by SHERIDAN, CHELSEA, MI, USA.**

10 9 8 7 6 5 4 3 2

MARVEL ADVENTURES FANTASTIC FOUR #10

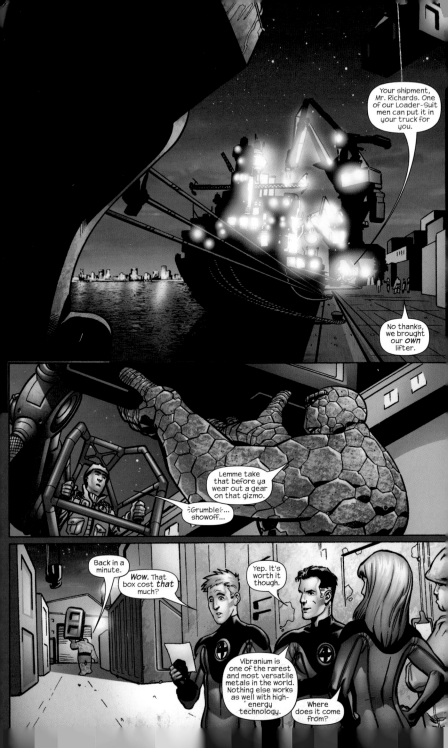

Franko sure came clean with a lot of info on this Vibranium smuggling operation. Good work, boys.

Yeah, but he didn't know where his gang is now, or when this big "supply raid" he kept yammerin' about is supposed to go down.

APPROACHING THE SUBCONTINENT IN 2 MINUTES.

You really think our coming out to apologize will help things?

I do. More importantly, we need to warn them of the attack coming.

And--we don't have a choice. The country doesn't acknowledge messages from outside its borders.

This is strange...

...we should be over the country right now, but I'm not picking up any readings of people or structures.

They must have some serious camouflage technology. Put us down by the edge of the jungle, Ben. We can look up close.

Please make sure yer seats and tray tables are in the upright n' locked position.

Where to first?

Hey, look!

Wow! This totally schools *Animal Planet*.

Do elephants usually roam by themselves?

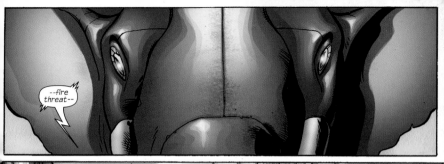

--fire threat--

--coat with non-combustible gel--

Ahgh! I'm always getting gooed!

Hey, that's no--

--elephant-- *whoa!* All right, buster, you're askin' for it!

Arrrhhh!

ZZZAAPZZZAAP

Whew!

Let him go, Ele-bot!

Everyone, into the jungle!

Where ya going, Reed?

Honey--? I don't think he's going by choice!

Hang on, I-- nuts, I still can't flame on!

Lousy goo!

I'll get him.

What happened?

Somebody swung me all around before I could even react! It must have been the Black Panther, he was so fast.

Untie my arm, will you?

So when we find this place, what are we going to saa-- AAAAAAAYYYY!!!

Johnny!

Put me down, dude!

Hang on, kid, I'll make 'im--

--drop ya.

Ya lousy-- ya tricked me! What is this muck?

It is quick-sand. Your friend can help you.

YOW!

Oof!

I gotcha, kid!

It's too late fer me, but you can still live!

No! Old buddy!

Tell Sue and Reed ta water my ficus...

≋Unf!≋ What's going on?

The King is exposed!

Get between them! We must protect T'Challa!

Stand *down*, Americans!

I've got flame again!

And I'm wearin' my Thing Fists!

No one do anything!

We're not here to fight!

Put down your weapons.

T'Challa commands.

VICTORY!

Wakanda's greatest champion is also her wisest king. Tradition and distrust kept the country apart from the world for many years. Yet the Black Panther realized that friendship should always be welcomed in his land.

Ask any citizen of this majestic land and you will hear this: Wakanda has no greater friends than those known as...

The Fantastic Four!

The End

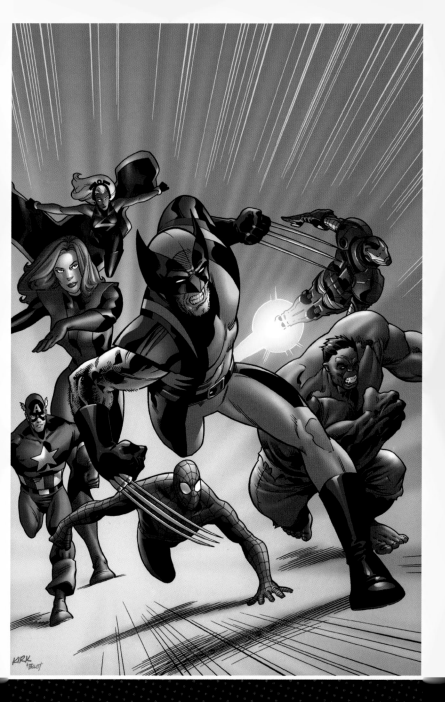

WOLVERINE

STORM

CAPTAIN AMERICA

SPIDER-MAN

HULK

GIANT-GIRL

Welcome back to "Mysteries of the Jungle"!

Tonight we're on the outskirts of Wakanda--a mysterious nation deep in the heart of Africa.

For centuries, there have been legends of a black panther that silently stalks this jungle, protecting the people of Wakanda.

Recent reports of a vicious cat-like creature causing chaos in this region have brought us here to uncover the truth behind the myth!

Is the black panther real? And is this legendary beast truly a "protector"... or just another predator?

WAKANDA WILD SIDE!

FERAL MUTANT BRAWLER. WEATHER GODDESS. SUPER-SOLDIER FROM WORLD WAR II. SPIDER-POWERED WEB-SLINGER. SUPER-STRONG ALTER EGO OF SCIENTIST BRUCE BANNER. GIANT-SIZED CRIMEFIGHTER. TOGETHER THEY ARE THE WORLD'S MIGHTIEST HEROES, BATTLING THE FOES THAT NO SINGLE SUPER HERO COULD WITHSTAND!

THE AVENGERS

Marc Sumerak writer Ig Guara pencils Jay Leisten inks Ulises Arreola color Dave Sharpe letters Kirk and Staples cover Joe Sabino production Nathan Cosby assistant editor Mark Paniccia editor Joe Quesada editor in chief Dan Buckley publisher

--though, *sadly*, there are still no signs of the show's *host* or *crew*.

⑤ TV CREW MISSING!

But judging by the *terrifying images* caught at the *end* of the tape...

RRRRRRRR

...they may have *found* the *mysterious creature* they were *searching* for...

Avengers Tower. **New York City.**

Whoa! Gross! Do you think a *panther* just *ate* that entire TV crew?

No. That *wasn't* no panther.

It was *someone* a lot *worse*...

"*Someone*"? What do you *mean*, Wolverine? You *recognize* that *thing*?

I'd *know* it *anywhere*, Spidey. And I'd do *anything* to *stop* it...

Where *claw man* going?

Hunting.

Giant-Girl?

The **nose** don't lie, sweet-heart.

I *don't* see anyone, boss man. It's just us!

Maybe it's *time* to take the *ol' sniffer* in for a tune-up...

sniff?

Maybe it's *time* to *stop* using baby shampoo.

But if we *really are* in *danger,* my *spider-sense* should be *going* nuts.

I *recommend* we keep a *low profile* until we can *figure out* what *Wolverine*--

Fine. Your nose still *works.*

And, by the way, I have *very sensitive eyes...*

Hulk not want *low* profile!

Hulk want to *find stupid cat man* and *smash him!*

Hulk! Wait!

TRIP!

Okay...

Uh oh.

CBROING!

While we **appreciate** your **hospitality**, King T'Challa, the **Avengers** are here on **serious business**.

Three men were recently **attacked** on the outskirts of **your nation** and--

The **men you seek** are **safe**, Captain.

In an **effort** to escape their **attacker**, they **crossed** the **Wakandan** border. My warriors **found them** and **brought them** to me.

While **my people** do not usually **burden themselves** with the **affairs** of the **outside world**, we are also **not so cold** as to **turn away** those in need.

And the **monster** that **ambushed** 'em? What did your **toy soldiers** do with **him**?

Nothing.

His **actions**, while **barbaric**, did not **take place** on **Wakandan** soil. Therefore, he is **not** our concern.

Even so, you must have **some information** that could **help us** in our **search** for Sabretooth.

His **capture** means **safety** for the **entire region**.

Wakanda is under the **protection** of the **Panther**, my dear. We fear **no one**.

As for those who **dwell outside** our **borders**...

...they are **on their own**.

So it **seems**...

KZZZAATT!

Nice save, Storm...

...but I had everything under control.

Of course you did.

Too scared to face me alone, Logan? Had to call in your super pals? Heh...looks like someone is getting soft...

There is no shame in depending on others, Sabretooth.

Hey, I ain't complainin'! The bigger the fight, the more fun for me!

Is that *all you got,* girl?

A little *bad weather* ain't gonna *stop* me!

I could take on *a whole army!*

CHUD!

You *heard him,* Stormy. And *last I checked,* those Wakandan soldier were pretty *eager* for a *good fight.*

But *T'Challa said* he did *not* want us to *bring our fight* to his *homeland.*

Your *old flame* just wanted *free rein* to *ignore the problem...*

...but he *won't be able* to if we take it to his *doorstep.*

By the *bright lady,* I hope you are *right...*

Hey! What're you *doin'*? Put me *down!*

...for *all of our sakes...*

We're *here* to help, Panther.

Clearly you are *not*...or your *mindless* battle would *never* have entered my borders!

T'Challa?!?

Not *too* proud to come *down* from yer *throne* and *fight* alongside the *commoners* after all?

This *conflict* has come to *my* *homeland*.

It is *my* responsibility now.

Sorry, pal. It was *my* fight first.

But *lucky* for you, I'm willing to *share!*

That's it! Keep *fightin'* each other, boys!

Makes my job *way* easier!

Shut yer jaws.

FWAM

Y'know, I used to be *just like* you, T'Chachi. A *loner*.

Wanted to *solve* all my problems *by myself*.

But *my time* with the Avengers is *teachin'* me somethin'...

You *"heroes"* have already put my *country* in *enough* danger.

Stand down! I shall *deal* with this *on my own!*

AVENGERS: EARTH'S MIGHTIEST HEROES #1

TRUST ME.

RUST

CHRISTOPHER YOST WRITER
PATRICK SCHERBERGER ARTIST
JEAN-FRANÇOIS BEAULIEU COLORIST
DAVE SHARPE LETTERER
TAYLOR ESPOSITO PRODUCTION
MICHAEL HORWITZ ASSISTANT EDITOR
NATHAN COSBY EDITOR
JOE QUESADA EDITOR IN CHIEF
DAN BUCKLEY PUBLISHER
ALAN FINE EXECUTIVE PRODUCER

KSHH!

KSSSH!

KSSSH!

KSSSH!

KSSSH!

...WELL, THAT'S JUST GREAT. THIS IS ALL YOUR FAULT, PANTHER.

DO YOU NOT HAVE FLARE ARROWS?

I USED THE LAST ONE SIGNALING YOU TO THIS PLACE.

MAN, I KNEW I SHOULD HAVE DONE THIS SOLO!! WHIPLASH COULD BE RIGHT IN FRONT OF ME AND I WOULDN'T KNOW IT.

HAWKEYE... TRUST ME.

TRUST *YOU?* THAT'S RICH. TRUST THE GUY THAT BROKE INTO AVENGERS MANSION AND SPIED ON THE TEAM?

WE'RE BOTH GOING TO *DIE HERE* AND YOU'RE PLAYING *GAMES!*

I WILL IGNORE THE FACT THAT *YOU* WERE A SPY FOR *S.H.I.E.L.D.*, BECAUSE EVEN MORE DANGEROUS ARE YOUR *EMOTIONS.*

YOU ARE RULED BY THEM! YOU ARE *RECKLESS,* AND LET YOUR EGO MAKE DECISIONS FOR YOU.

BUT PERHAPS WE SHOULD *BOTH* LEARN TO TRUST, IF WE ARE GOING TO BE ON A TEAM TOGETHER.

END.

00:00:00:01

MARVEL UNIVERSE AVENGERS

HAWKEYE APPRECIATES *STEALTH*, BUT HE'S UNDERCOVER IN THE RINGMASTER'S *CIRCUS OF CRIME.*

BLACK WIDOW IS AN INFILTRATION EXPERT, BUT SHE'S SHUTTING DOWN THE TASKMASTER'S SUPER VILLAIN ACADEMY.

IT'S LIKE YOU *WANT* ME TO SMASH YOU.

DING

ANT-MAN AND WASP ARE IDEAL FOR *QUIET* RAIDS, BUT THEY'RE DISARMING COUNT NEFARIA AND MADAME MASQUE.

WHOA!

PLEASE LET ME TAKE THESE GUYS OUT.

NO NEED!

OOF!

NUMBER 407, WHO WAS IN THE ELEVATOR?

FALSE ALARM. AN AUTOMATIC PROGRAM, *NOTHING* MORE.

SIX MINUTES. WE MUST MOVE *FASTER.* PLEASE TRY TO KEEP UP.

OKAY, THAT'S IT, PUSS N' BOOTS. I DON'T CARE ABOUT ANY MADBOMB.

I'M MAD ENOUGH RIGHT NOW!

HRRAR!

AND THAT'S THE *END* OF THIS LITTLE *JOY BUZZER*.

BETTER CHECK ON *SYLVESTER*.

IS THAT ALL? SURELY YOU CANNOT HAVE GIVEN UP! WHO ELSE IS PREPARED FOR ANNIHILATION?!

SNAP OUT OF IT, GARFIELD. MINDLESS VIOLENCE IS MY THING, YOU STICK TO *"STRATEGY"* OR WHATEVER.

HULK? THANK YOU. I AM AFRAID I LOST CONTROL OF MYSELF.

REGARDLESS, THE CITY IS *SAVED*. BY WORKING TOGETHER AS A *TEAM*, WE STOPPED THE THREAT OF THE *MADBOMB* WITHOUT DOING *DAMAGE* TO THIS *MAGNIFICENT* STRUCTURE.

WELL... NOT *TOO MUCH* DAMAGE, ANYWAY.

HIS SKILLED FINGERS MANIPULATING A HIDDEN LOCK, THE DARK-CLAD *PANTHER* OPENS THE DOMED SKY-LIGHT, AND--

LUCKILY, I LEARNED THIS *ALTERNATE* MANNER OF ENTRANCE FROM *CAPTAIN AMERICA*--

...AFTER OUR RECENT CLASH WITH THE IMPOSTOR WHO CLAIMED TO BE *ZEMO!* *

*AS TRIUMPHANTLY CHRONICLED IN THE PREMIERE ISH OF CAP'S OWN MAG! ---STAN THE MAN.

BUT, THERE IS STILL SOME *MYSTERY* HERE... WHICH MUST BE SWIFTLY *SOLVED!*

I *RADIOED* THE AVENGERS OF MY ARRIVAL IN NEW YORK ONLY AN *HOUR* AGO, AND...

WAIT! THAT ALMOST IMPERCEPT-IBLE *SOUND*..!

THE NEXT SECOND, ONLY THE WAKANDA CHIEFTAIN'S LIGHTNING-FAST *REFLEXES* SAVE HIM FROM INSTANTANE-OUS *DOOM*, AS--

DEADLY *LASERS*... STRIKING THE VERY SPOT WHERE I *STOOD* BUT A MOMENT AGO!

ONLY ONE WITH THE *SPEED* OF THE BOUNDING *CHEETAH* COULD HAVE EVADED THEM!

IS *THIS* HOW THE AVENGERS GREET THOSE WHO COME TO *JOIN* THEM...

...WITH BEAMS DESIGNED TO *DESTROY??*

BUT, *NO!* STEVE ROGERS TOLD ME ALL THEIR GUARDIAN DEVICES ARE SET ONLY TO *STUN!*

STILL, I SHALL LEARN WHO HAS *ACTIVATED* THEM AGAINST ME--

...AS SOON AS I LEAP OVER THESE RAYS TO *FREEDOM!*

YET, ALMOST AT ONCE--- THIS IS *MADDENING!*

I'M STILL IN SOME SORT OF *TUNNEL*... WRAPPED IN *DARKNESS!*

STILL, THE FAINTEST GLEAM OF LIGHT IS A SHINING *BEACON* TO MY EYES!

I SHALL *FOLLOW* THE TUNNEL --- NO MATTER *WHERE* IT LEADS!

2.

THEN, SUDDENLY, BEFORE A SINGLE *STEP* CAN BE TAKEN...

I'M *CAUGHT*... BETWEEN TWO LARGE *TUBES!*

THAK!

ANOTHER OF THE AVENGER *PROTECTIVE* DEVICES... MENTIONED BY *CAPTAIN AMERICA...* ...WHICH I *FORGOT*, IN MY HASTE!

THIS ONE, HOWEVER, POSES NO MENACE... BUT IS MEANT MERELY TO *RESTRAIN!*

IT ALSO SERVES AS A *SHAFT*... THRU WHICH I CAN SPEEDILY REACH THE VERY *NERVE CENTER* OF THE BUILDING!

BY BRACING MY BACK AGAINST ITS SIDES AS I MOVE, I CAN REACH THE *BOTTOM* WITHIN SECONDS...

...WHERE THE TRANSPARENT PLEXIGLASS IS AT ITS *WEAKEST!*

KRAASH!

AND, NO MATTER *WHAT* LIES BEYOND... THE *PANTHER* IS READY!

BUT, EVEN ONE WHO HAS FACED THE RAMPAGING *LION*... WHO HAS FOUGHT *SATANIC* FOES ALONGSIDE THE *FANTASTIC FOUR*... IS UNPREPARED FOR WHAT *NEXT* GREETS HIS STARTLED EYES...

WHAT IN THE NAME OF THE TIMELESS *JUNGLE* WHICH SPAWNED ME..?

IT'S... *UN- BELIEVABLE!!*

3.

THE AVENGERS... **DEAD!!**

INSTANTLY, THE AGILE AFRICAN LEAPS TO THE SIDE OF THE *NEAREST* UNMOVING FORM...

I DARED HOPE I WAS *WRONG*...

THAT, SOME-HOW, IN THE GLOOMY DARK-NESS, MY EYES HAD *DECEIVED* ME...MY JUNGLE-TRAINED SENSES *ERRED!*

BUT, THERE IS NO *PULSE*... NO SLIGHTEST *BREATH*..!

HOLD! SOMEONE JUST *ENTERED* THE ROOM!

WHO..??

A MOMENT LATER, BRILLIANT *LIGHT* FLOODS THE CHAMBER... BEFORE EVEN THE *PANTHER* CAN REACT...

SOME SORT OF *WEAPON*... AIMED TOWARDS ME!

IN MY CONCERN, I WAS *CARELESS!*

THAT YOU *WERE*, MY MYSTERIOUS MASKED FRIEND...

AND NOW, NO AMOUNT OF *FALSE* ANXIETY WILL PULL THE WOOL OVER THE EYES OF AN *AGENT* OF *SHIELD!*

YOU'RE HEREBY *UNDER ARREST*...FOR THE *MURDER* OF THOSE THREE AVENGERS!

BUT, I ARRIVED HERE ONLY SECONDS BEFORE *YOU* DID...AND *DISCOVERED* THEM, JUST AS THEY ARE...!

BEFORE YOU GO ON, IT'S MY *DUTY* TO WARN YOU OF YOUR CONSTITUTIONAL *RIGHTS!*

SAVE YOUR *EXCUSES!* *JASPER SITWELL* WASN'T BORN YESTERDAY!

STAND AGAINST THE *WALL*...WHILE I CONTACT THE *POLICE!*

4.

Panel 1 (top left): STUNNED INTO MOMENTARY *INACTION*, THE JUNGLE PRINCE DOES AS HE IS BIDDEN, AND, WITHIN ONE MINUTE...

I'M AFRAID YOU HEARD ME *CORRECTLY*, INSPECTOR!

I DIDN'T ACTUALLY *WITNESS* THE MURDER!

BUT, I'VE APPREHENDED THE *KILLER*...A HOODED ASSASSIN WHO CALLS HIMSELF...THE *PANTHER*!

NO, *I* NEVER HEARD OF HIM, *EITHER*!

IT WOULD BE A SIMPLE FEAT TO *WREST* MY CAPTOR'S GUN FROM HIM...!

YET, I SENSE THAT MY BEST RECOURSE IS A *WAITING GAME*!

Panel 2 (top right): HOWEVER, THE PAIR ARE NOT KEPT WAITING FOR *LONG*...

ALL RIGHT, SONNY, YOU CAN PUT AWAY THAT FANCY *POPGUN* NOW!

WE'LL TAKE OVER---NOW THAT YOU TURNED OFF THE AVENGERS' GIZMOS TO LET US *IN*!

I'D PREFER TO BE ADDRESSED AS *AGENT SITWELL*, INSPECTOR...RATHER THAN *SONNY*!

THE SITUATION IS WELL IN HAND...BUT I'M *GLAD* YOU'RE *HERE*!

THAT *STORY* YOU HANDED OUT ON THE PHONE...WAS IT ON THE *LEVEL*?

IT *COULDN'T* HAVE BEEN!

WHO WOULD HAVE *DARED* ATTACK THEM...IN THEIR OWN *HEADQUARTERS*?

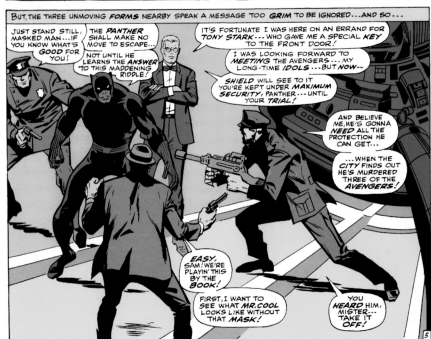

Panel 3 (bottom): BUT, THE THREE UNMOVING *FORMS* NEARBY SPEAK A MESSAGE TOO *GRIM* TO BE IGNORED...AND SO...

JUST STAND STILL, MASKED MAN...IF YOU KNOW WHAT'S *GOOD* FOR YOU!

THE *PANTHER* SHALL MAKE NO MOVE TO ESCAPE...NOT UNTIL HE LEARNS THE *ANSWER* TO THIS MADDENING RIDDLE!

IT'S FORTUNATE I WAS HERE ON AN ERRAND FOR *TONY STARK*---WHO GAVE ME A SPECIAL *KEY* TO THE FRONT DOOR!

I WAS LOOKING FORWARD TO *MEETING* THE AVENGERS...MY LONG-TIME *IDOLS*...BUT NOW--

SHIELD WILL SEE TO IT YOU'RE KEPT UNDER *MAXIMUM SECURITY*, PANTHER---UNTIL YOUR *TRIAL*!

AND BELIEVE ME, HE'S GONNA *NEED* ALL THE PROTECTION HE CAN GET...

...WHEN THE *CITY* FINDS OUT HE'S MURDERED THREE OF THE *AVENGERS*!

EASY, SAM! WE'RE PLAYIN' THIS BY THE *BOOK*!

FIRST, I WANT TO SEE WHAT *MR. COOL* LOOKS LIKE WITHOUT THAT *MASK*!

YOU *HEARD* HIM, MISTER...TAKE IT *OFF*!

5

BUT, EVEN AS T'CHALLA *THINKS*, THE WORLD AT LARGE *HEARS*...AND *JUDGES*...

...HERE'S A *NEWS FLASH*...RECEIVED BY THIS STATION ONLY *MOMENTS* AGO...!

THREE OF THE FAMED *AVENGERS*... ARE *DEAD!*

A MYSTERIOUS MASKED FIGURE HAS BEEN *ARRESTED* AT THE SCENE OF THE CRIME...A MAN WHO CALLS HIMSELF THE *PANTHER!*

HE..HE'S *KIDDIN'!* HE'S *GOTTA* BE!

YET, IT IS SOON OBVIOUS TO STARTLED VIEWERS EVERYWHERE THAT THIS IS *NO HOAX*...

...I *REPEAT*: THE AVENGERS KNOWN AS *HAWKEYE, GOLIATH,* AND THE *WASP* ARE DEAD... APPARENTLY *MURDERED*...!

IT ISN'T *POSSIBLE!* I SAW THEM ONLY *DAYS* AGO... HELPED HANK PYM REGAIN HIS *GROWING* POWERS!

STARK LAB. INC.

MUST FINISH THESE DELICATE ADJUSTMENTS ON MY *TEST-ROBOT* RIGHT AWAY!...

..SO I CAN INVESTIGATE... AS *IRON MAN!*

ELSEWHERE, IN A DARKENED ALLEYWAY, A STAR-SPANGLED SENTINEL HEARS THE INCREDIBLE NEWS ON A *CAR RADIO*...

HANK... JAN... HAWKEYE... ALL *KILLED* IN ONE FELL SWOOP?

AND, THE *PANTHER*... AN ACCUSED *ASSASSIN?*

I JUST RETURNED FROM BATTLING THE *SLEEPER*... INTENDED TO VISIT THEM...WHEN I STOPPED TO BATTLE THESE *PETTY THUGS!*

AND NOW, THEY'RE *DEAD!* ...AND MY NEW-FOUND FRIEND BELIEVED *GUILTY?!*

WITHIN THE HOUR, A *SPECIAL EDITION* STOPS EVEN THE NOBLE *GOD OF THUNDER*...

THEIRS WERE THE SPIRITS THAT KEPT THE NAME OF THE AVENGERS *ALIVE*...

...TILL *THEY* THEM-SELVES WERE--- NO *MORE!*

EXTRA DAILY
3 AVENGERS MURDERED!

WOULD THAT THIS DREAD NIGHT HAD NE'ER *FALLEN!*

HOWEVER, SOMEWHERE IN THE STUNNED CITY, *ONE* VOICE THERE IS WHICH IS RAISED IN EXULTANT *TRIUMPH*...

MY PLAN *SUCCEEDED*... TO THE FINAL *DETAIL!*

THAT WHICH HAS BEEN DULY SOWN, SHALL NOW BE *HARVESTED*, BY THE MAN WHO *KILLED* THE TRIO OF AVENGERS...

I... THE *GRIM REAPER!!*

7.

FOR THE PRESENT, IT SUITS MY SCHEME THAT THE LUCKLESS *PANTHER* BE THOUGHT THE MURDERER...FOR, THOSE THREE DEATHS ARE ONLY THE *FIRST* I SHALL ACCOMPLISH!

AND, THE SUPREME *IRONY* OF ALL IS THAT THE *TRUE* MURDERERS SHALL BE... THE *AUTHORITIES* THEMSELVES...

...IN A WAY THAT THEY CAN SCARCELY *IMAGINE!!*

THEN, AS A STARTLED NATION *GRIEVES*...AND AS THE PREVIOUS PANEL'S ENIGMATIC *WORDS* YET RING IN OUR EARS ...THE VENEMOUS *GRIM REAPER* LETS HIS THOUGHTS STRAY BACK A MERE *HOUR* IN TIME...

THERE IS THE HATED BUILDING WHICH I SEEK... DIRECTLY *BELOW!*

MY ATTACK MUST BE *SUDDEN...SWIFT...* TOTALLY *UNEXPECTED!*

AND, IT MUST BEGIN... *NOW!*

IN HIS MIND'S EYE, HE SEES A HEAVILY REINFORCED *WALL* LOOM BEFORE HIS JET-EQUIPPED PLATFORM... RELIVES AGAIN THE MOMENT WHEN HE LIFTED HIS WEIRD, OMINOUS *SCYTHE*, AND...

SHOOO...

WHAT IN THE NAME OF...??

SOMEBODY... JUST BLASTED A KING-SIZE *HOLE*...IN OUR WALL!

BUT...WE'RE SEVERAL STORIES *HIGH...!*

THE ELEMENT OF *SURPRISE*, FOOLS...MY *SECOND* MOST POTENT WEAPON!

THE *OTHER* YOU SHALL LEARN IN A MOMENT...

...WHEN THE *GRIM REAPER* WREAKS HIS AWESOME *VENGEANCE!*

VENGEANCE? YOU MUST BE SOME KIND'A FULL-TIME *PSYCHO!*

NONE OF US EVER LAID *EYES* ON YOU BEFORE!

GOTTA *STALL* 'IM FOR A FEW SECONDS!

HANK AND JAN WERE *HIT* HARDER BY THE EXPLOSION THAN I WAS...AND NEED A CHANCE TO *RECOVER!*

8

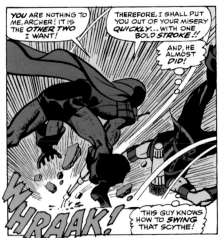

YOU ARE NOTHING TO ME, ARCHER! IT IS THE *OTHER TWO* I WANT!

THEREFORE, I SHALL PUT YOU OUT OF YOUR MISERY *QUICKLY*... WITH ONE BOLD *STROKE!!*

AND, HE ALMOST *DID!*

WHRAAK!

THIS GUY KNOWS HOW TO *SWING* THAT SCYTHE!

BAH! NO MERE AMATEURISH *ACROBATICS* WILL SAVE YOU FROM THE *GRIM REAPER!*

WE *HEARD* YOUR NAME ALREADY, MELVIN!

JUST BE SURE AN' *SIGN* OUR *GUEST BOOK...* ON YOUR WAY *OUT!*

BRAZZT!

SHEESH! THAT THING EVEN FIRES *ELECTRIC BEAMS!*

ONE INCH *CLOSER*, AND WE'D BE HAVIN' *TOASTED* BOW-SLINGER!

YOU'VE *DONE* YOUR BIT, HAWKEYE! NOW, LET OL' *HIGH-POCKETS* HAVE A WHIRL!

GOLIATH!!

WATCH OUT FOR THAT *PIG-STICKER* OF HIS, MAN-MOUNTAIN!

I'M BETTIN' IT'S GOT MORE *GIZMOS* THAN I'VE GOT *ARROWS!*

YOU WERE EXPECTING MAYBE *LUCY IN THE SKY WITH DIAMONDS?*

DON'T *WORRY*, LITTLE BUDDY!

I'VE FOUGHT THIS KIND *BEFORE*... AND ALWAYS COME OUT ON *TOP!*

THAT YOU *HAVE*, HENRY PYM... BY COMMITTING THE TREACHEROUS DEEDS OF A *PROVEN MURDERER!!*

HAH! YOU ARE *STARTLED* TO HEAR YOURSELF CALLED BY THAT NAME YOU SO RICHLY *DESERVE!*

AND, THAT SINGLE MOMENT OF *HESITATION* IS ALL I NEED... TO *ESCAPE* YOUR OVERRATED GRASP!

9.

...AND, BOTH THE MURDERER CALLED *GOLIATH*... AND HE WHO WOULD *PROTECT* HIM... ARE IRREVOCABLY *DOOMED!*

A *WIDE-SPREAD* ELECTRICAL CHARGE ---CATCHING US *BOTH!*

OUR ONLY CHANCE NOW... IS *JAN!*

BLACKING OUT...! CAN'T STAND... THE SEARING *PAIN!!*

ZZAKT KAZZAKKAK

BUT, THE LOVELY AVENGING *HEIRESS* IS NOT SPARED THE FATE OF HER CLOSEST COMRADES...

HANK AND HAWKEYE... DIDN'T KNOW I WAS *FLYING* JUST ABOVE THEM!

THAT CHARGE *OVERCAME*... MY MENTAL SIZE-CONTROL! I'M... GROWING *LARGER* AGAIN...!

ZZIKK!

THEN, AS THE *LAST* OF THE TRIO SLUMPS INTO UN-CONSCIOUS-NESS...

YOU CANNOT *HEAR* ME... *ANY* OF YOU...

YET, I AM THE *ONE* FOE YOU HAD NO *CHANCE* AGAINST!

FOR, I AM THE EMBODIMENT OF *DEATH*... AND I STRUCK IN THE NAME OF JUST *VENGEANCE!*

"IF YOU COULD HEAR ME, I WOULD ASK YOU TO REMEMBER ONE CALLED... *WONDER MAN*...!*"

GET *HIM!* HE'S AN AGENT OF *ZEMO!*

*OUR ONCE-IN-A-LIFETIME HERO-VILLAIN FROM ISH #9! --- SMILEY.

"*YES*, FOOLS... *WONDER MAN!* HE WHO BECAME VIRTUALLY AN *AVENGER*... IN ORDER TO *DESTROY* YOU FROM WITHIN ---"

YOU *MISSED*, GIANT-MAN... BUT I SHALL *NOT!*

THOUGH YOU *DWARF* ME, I'M AT LEAST YOUR *EQUAL* IN POWER!

11.

"IN EVERY WAY, HE PROVED *MIGHTIER* THAN THE ONES WHO OPPOSED HIM! YET, BY SOME *TRICKERY*, HE WAS *DEFEATED... POISONED!*"

"AND THOSE WHO CALLED THEMSELVES *AVENGERS* STOOD BY AND WATCHED HIM *DIE*...AND DID *NOTHING* TO SAVE HIM...!"

"THIS I *KNOW*, FOR SIMON WILLIAMS... WONDER MAN... WAS MY *BROTHER!*"

THE NEXT MOMENT, ALL THE VENEMOUS RANCOR IN HIS SOUL POURED OUT, THE *GRIM REAPER* GESTURES ONCE MORE WITH HIS MYSTERIOUS *SCYTHE*, AND...

THAT WHICH MY WEAPON HAS DONE, IT CAN *UNDO!*

ITS *ELECTRICAL POWER* SHALL NOW *RESTORE* THIS CHAMBER!

FOR, I HAVE *PLANS* IN MIND...PLANS THAT SHALL DESTROY THE *OTHERS* WHO LET MY BROTHER DIE...!

HOWEVER, WE'LL HAVE TO LET THE TANGLED SKEIN OF FATE *REMAIN* TWISTED A BIT LONGER...AS, RETURNING TO THE *PRESENT*--

IF HE'S REALLY AN *AFRICAN PRINCE* LIKE HE SAYS, WE CAN'T *BOOK* HIM!

THIS'D BE A JOB FOR THE *U.N.!*

SURE...BUT WE'VE GOT JUST *HIS* WORD ON THAT!

I CAN'T FIND THIS *WAKANDA* PLACE ON ANY MAP!

NOR *SHALL* HE...FOR ITS LOCATION IS *SECRET!*

BUT, I'VE ACCOMPLISHED MY *PURPOSE* IN ALLOWING MYSELF TO BE BROUGHT HERE...

AND NOW, IT IS TIME FOR THE *PANTHER* TO PROWL THE CITY ONCE MORE...

...TO LEARN IF THE GNAWING *SUSPICION* WHICH FILLS MY MIND... IS THE SENSES-STAGGERING *TRUTH!*

KRAAASH!

HE'S MAKING A *BREAK* FOR IT!

AND HE MOVES LIKE *GREASED LIGHTNING!*

12

WITHIN MOMENTS, A GASPING, GAPING *CROWD* HAS FORMED ON THE STREETS OUTSIDE THE STATION... CREATING A *SECOND* HAZARD FOR THE POLICE...

THE GUY WE HEARD ABOUT ON TV--HE'S GETTING AWAY!

WHILE HE'S ON THE LOOSE, *NOBODY'S* SAFE!

IF ONLY THAT *SHIELD* AGENT HADN'T CUT OUT SO SOON... *WAIT!!*

THERE'S THE PANTHER--ON THAT *LEDGE!*

I HAD HOPED TO *ELUDE* THEM... BY SCALING THIS ALMOST SHEER *WALL!*

BUT *NOW*...

KTAHK

YOU'RE *TRAPPED,* PANTHER... SO *SURRENDER!*

THIS IS THE ONLY *WARNING BURST* YOU'RE GETTING!

PTHKK

BRAKKA

THE POLICE HAVE HIM *CORNERED!* HE'S *GOTTA* GIVE UP, OR... *LOOK!!*

HE---HE'S *JUMPING...* TOWARDS THE NEXT *BUILDING!*

HE LEAPS LIKE SOME *JUNGLE BEAST*... LIKE A *REAL* PANTHER!

BUT, IT'S *TOO FAR!* NOTHING THAT *LIVES* COULD JUMP THAT DISTANCE--!

FOR A FLEETING ETERNITY, THE HORRIFIED SPECTATORS AND POLICE BELOW HOLD THEIR *BREATH*... WHILE, HIGH ABOVE, TAUT MUSCLES *STRAIN,* ACHINGLY...

AND *THEN*...

HE MADE IT!!

THERE ARE A *DOZEN* EXITS FROM THAT BUILDING! WE'LL NEVER COVER THEM ALL *IN TIME!*

THE MAN WHO MURDERED THE AVENGERS... HAS *ESCAPED!!*

13

Panel 1:

BUT, MINUTES LATER, AS A JUNGLE *JUGGERNAUT* RACES THRU THE BACK ALLEYS OF NEW YORK...

THE CROWDS ARE *WRONG!* THE AVENGERS' KILLER *HASN'T* ESCAPED!

NOR *SHALL* HE.. WHILE THE *PANTHER* IS FREE TO STALK HIM!

AND, I BELIEVE I KNOW JUST WHERE HE *IS!*

--BEHIND THE VAULTED *DOOR* THAT WOULD NOT OPEN--

--IN *AVENGERS HQ* ITSELF!

Panel 2:

A SHORT TIME LATER, IN *ANOTHER* PART OF THE SPRAWLING CITY...

SOON...VERY SOON... THE OTHERS WHOM I SEEK WILL COME TO ME... AND I SHALL BE *WAITING...*

HERE, IN THE *AVENGERS'* OWN SECRET-STUDDED MANSION!

*THOR...IRON MAN..CAPTAIN AMERICA...*ALL MUST FALL BEFORE MY DEATH-DISPENSING *SCYTHE!*

ONLY THEN CAN THE SOUL OF MY *BROTHER, WONDER MAN,* REST IN PEACE!

Panel 3:

SO *THAT'S* YOUR MOTIVE... AN IN-SANE *REVENGE!*

AND, TO CARRY IT OUT, YOU'VE DEVISED A WEAPON WHICH CHILLS THE VERY *SOUL!*

BUT, I FOUND ANOTHER *ENTRANCE* HERE--ONE SUCH AS ONLY *I* COULD USE!

THE *PANTHER!!*

Panel 4:

YES, ASSASSIN... THE *PANTHER,* HE WHOM YOU WISHED TO *DIE* FOR YOUR UNSPEAKABLE CRIME!

BUT NOW, *WHO-EVER* YOU MAY BE, YOU'LL *PAY* FOR YOUR OWN DEEDS!

FLZT!

FOOL! KEEP *AWAY* FROM ME!

I AM THE *GRIM REAPER...* MINE IS THE *SACRED SCYTHE* OF *JUSTICE..!*

14

JUSTICE, MY FRIEND?

PERHAPS... THE CRAZED JUSTICE OF A MADMAN!

DON'T... STRIKE ME... PLEASE!

I DID ONLY... WHAT I HAD TO DO...!

THEN, RISE...AND I'LL TURN YOU OVER TO THE AUTHORITIES FOR TREATMENT!

I HAVE NO DESIRE TO DO BATTLE WITH A TWISTED MIND...!

UNNHHH!

BUT, A SINGLE HEARTBEAT LATER...

THIS, THEN, IS THE WORTH OF A PLEDGE IN THE PLACE WHICH MEN CALL CIVILIZED!

A TREACHEROUS BLOW... THAT FEW COULD HAVE AVOIDED!

DID YOU TRULY THINK TO HUMBLE ME, DOLT...

I, WHOSE SCYTHE HOLDS THE POWER TO SLAY A THOUSAND COSTUMED CLOWNS?

AS LONG AS HE HOLDS THAT SHARP-BLADED WEAPON, THE ADVANTAGE IS HIS!

MUST TAUNT HIM...CAUSE HIM TO ACT EVER MORE RECKLESSLY!

YOU SPOKE OF AVENGING YOUR BROTHER'S DEATH, REAPER!

YET, THE OFFICIAL REPORT SAID HE WAS KILLED BY ZEMO...

...AND THAT HE DIED SAVING THE AVENGERS!

SLASH!

15.

AND, IN AN INCREDIBLY *SHORT* SPAN OF TIME...

THE BODIES WERE SENT TO THIS *HOSPITAL*...

...AS IF SOMEONE *SENSED* THE UNCANNY NATURE OF THEIR SUPPOSED *DEATHS!*

STILL, NO ONE WOULD ACCEPT *MY* STORY---THE TALE OF AN ACCUSED *MURDERER--!*

THUS, THE *PANTHER* MUST ACT OUT THIS LIFE-AND-DEATH DRAMA...*ALONE!*

IF ONLY THE *THREE* AVENGERS ARE TRULY ON THE *TOP FLOOR*... AS THE RADIO REPORTS SAID..!

SMAASH!

CHARLIE...*LOOK!* THAT *PANTHER* GUY... HERE JUST LIKE THEY *SAID* HE MIGHT BE!

BUT, HE'S MOVIN' TOO *FAST* FOR ME TO GET A BEAD ON HIM WITH THIS SPECIAL *RIFLE!*

MAYBE SO...BUT HE'S HEADIN' STRAIGHT FOR THE *AVENGERS!*

AND, THERE'S NO WAY *OUTTA* THAT ROOM... SO WE GOT 'IM!

THERE THEY ARE... BEHIND THIS THICK *DOOR*, AS I SUSPECTED!

BUT, THEY LIE SO *STILL*... THEIR FACES LIKE DREAD MASKS OF *DEATH!*

DID MY *MANIACAL* FOE MERELY *TAUNT* ME WHEN HE SAID THEY *LIVED?*

KRAKK!

18

HE CAN'T ESCAPE NOW!

WHY'D HE COME BACK---TO CERTAIN DEATH?

WHO CARES? THE IMPORTANT THING IS...HE'S TRAPPED!

BUT, WHAT'S HE DOING WITH THAT NUTTY BLADE? THAK!

I ONLY HOPE I'VE GUESSED CORRECTLY... AND THAT THIS ELECTRICAL CHARGE WILL NEUTRALIZE THE SCYTHE'S DEATH-DEALING EFFECTS!

IF I'M WRONG, WE SHALL ALL HAVE DIED IN VAIN...

...AND THE GRIM REAPER SHALL HAVE GAINED HIS MADDENED VENGEANCE!

BRAKKA

THE NEXT MOMENT, HIS POWERS DRAINED AT LAST BY HIS THROBBING SHOULDER, THE PANTHER LURCHES TO A STOP...

NOW WE'VE GOT 'IM! LET 'IM HAVE IT--!

HEY! WHAT IN BLUE BLAZES..??

THWOK!

SKRAK!

AN ARROW... SPLINTERING MY PISTOL!

BUT, ONLY ONE PERSON CAN SHOOT LIKE THAT, AND HE'S...

DEAD? DON'T YOU BELIEVE IT, BLUE BOYS!

THEN, THOSE ELECTRICAL BURSTS AWAKENED YOU... ALMOST INSTANTLY!

WE'VE BEEN ALIVE ALL ALONG... BUT, TILL NOW, WE COULDN'T MOVE!

BUT HOW..?

WE'LL FILL YOU IN ON THE DETAILS... AS SOON AS WE'RE SURE OF THEM OURSELVES!

RIGHT NOW, IT LOOKS LIKE WE'VE GOT A WOUNDED RESCUER TO TAKE CARE OF..! 19

QUICKLY, THE PANTHER PROVIDES THE BRIEFEST OF *EXPLANATIONS*...AND, SHORTLY AFTERWARD...

THE *GRIM REAPER*...GONE! THEN, HE WASN'T *DYING*, AFTER ALL!

HE MERELY SENSED *DEFEAT*...AND FAKED A MORTAL WOUND TO AVOID *CAPTURE!*

IF I EVER GET MY *MITTS* ON THAT *SICKLE-SWINGIN'* CREEP...

NO NEED TO DRAW US A *PICTURE*, PARTNER!

I'VE GOT A HUNCH YOU'LL GET ANOTHER *CRACK* AT HIM...BEFORE *LONG!*

BUT SOON, EVEN SUCH THOUGHTS OF *RETRIBUTION* ARE TEMPORARILY SHELVED...AS AN HISTORIC *EVENT* TAKES PLACE...

...AND SO, WITH ALL MEMBERS PRESENT...AND *CAPTAIN AMERICA*...VOTING *AYE*, I DECLARE THE DECISION *UNANIMOUS!*

T'CHALLA, SON OF T'CHAKA... WELCOME TO THE *AVENGERS!*

CAP RADIOED US ALL *ABOUT* YOU, T'CHALLA!

NOW WE'RE *BACK* TO *FIGHTING STRENGTH* AGAIN!

I SHALL ALWAYS STRIVE TO BE *WORTHY* OF HIM WHOM I *REPLACE*, JANET VAN DYNE!

YET, WHAT OF THE *OTHERS* OF WHOM I HAVE HEARD...*HERCULES*... *QUICKSILVER*...THE *SCARLET WITCH!*

THE *SON OF ZEUS* HAS RETURNED TO TIMELESS OLYMPUS...JUST AS *THOR, IRON MAN*, AND *CAP* RESIGNED TO PURSUE THEIR OWN PRIVATE DESTINIES!

ALL THE NAMES OF THOSE WHO HAVE BEEN AVENGERS ARE ENSHRINED IN *GLORY*...UNMATCHED IN THE *ANNALS* OF *ADVENTURE!*

...ALL SAVE *TWO*...THOSE OF *WANDA* AND *PIETRO!*

TO *FIND* THEM...TO LEARN IF THEY ARE NOW *FRIEND* OR *FOE*...THAT IS THE *TASK* WE MUST NOW SET OUR-SELVES!

THEN, LET THE WORD GO FORTH...THAT TODAY, YOU HAVE GAINED A NEW *ALLY*...

ONE WHO HAS GIVEN UP A *THRONE*, THAT HE MAY BETTER SERVE A *GREATER KINGDOM*...THE WHOLE OF *MANKIND* ITSELF!

FOR, NOW THE *PANTHER* IS TRULY AN *AVENGER!!*

NEXT ISH: PERHAPS THE MOST TOTALLY UNEXPECTED *FOES* OF ALL... *THE EXTRAORDINARY* X-MEN!

20.

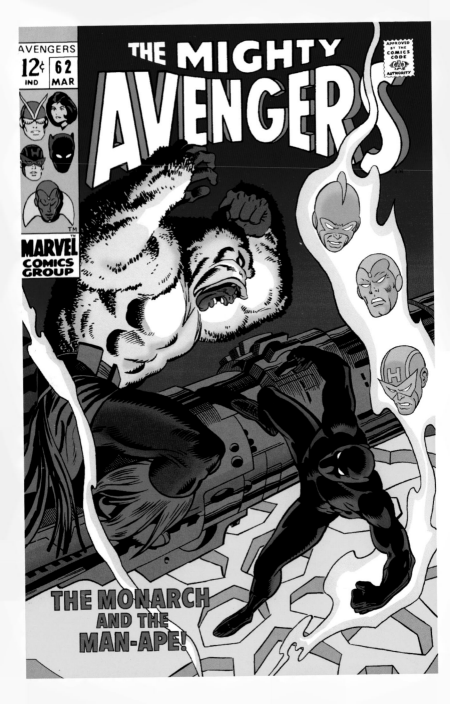

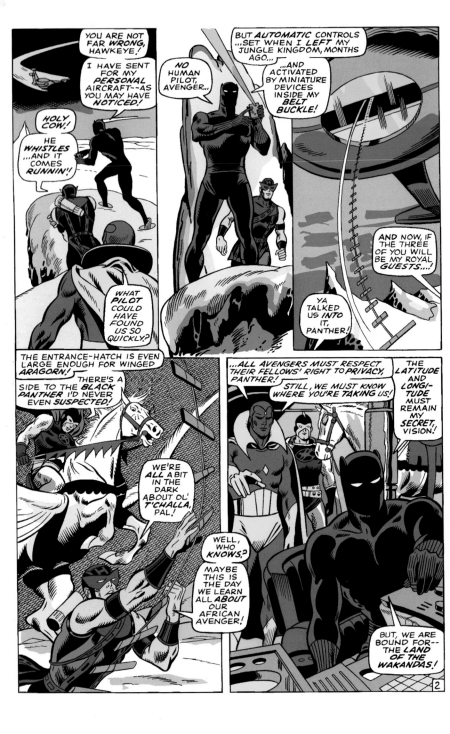

THEN, SUDDENLY, AS A *VERDANT* PATCH OF *JUNGLE* YAWNS BENEATH THE SHIP...

WE WERE IN *AFRICA* ALL THE TIME!

BUT, THAT *ICE*--THE *BITING COLD*--!

THEY WERE BUT REMINDERS OF *YMIR*, BOWMAN...THE *ICE MONSTER* WE *VANQUISHED!*

BUT NOW, *BRACE YOURSELVES!*

WE ARE GOING... *DOWN!!*

GREAT MERLIN!

THE JUNGLE FLOOR *PARTED*... AND WE WERE LOWERED INTO A *MECHANIZED WONDERLAND!*

MY HUMBLE THANKS FOR THE *COMPLIMENT*, BLACK KNIGHT!

THE PROUD WAKANDA *DO*, INDEED, DWELL IN PART WITHIN A *MAN-MADE* JUNGLE!

NO MAN--WHITE *OR* BLACK--GAINS ADMITTANCE TO OUR LAND UNLESS WE *DESIRE* IT!

3

4

ONE OF THEM *ESCAPES!*

FIRE!

YES, LOOK--AND, IF YOUR EYES ARE *FAST* ENOUGH-- YOU'LL SEE YOUR PUNY BULLETS *SHATTER* ON MY ANDROID FRAME!

NOW *I'LL* JOIN THE FRAY-- WITH MY *EBONY BLADE!*

BUT, *NONE* OF THIS MAKES ANY *SENSE!*

SHOTS-- OUTSIDE THE *SHIP!*

WHATEVER THEIR *SOURCE--* WHATEVER THEIR *CAUSE* --THEY MUST *CEASE!*

WE ARE FIRING, BUT-- *LOOK!*

WOULD SOME MAD *FOOL* UNDO THE WORK OF *YEARS?*

HALT!!

NO! IT CANNOT *BE!*

IT'S--*PRINCE T'CHALLA!* THE *BLACK PANTHER* HAS RETURNED!

AND RETURNED *ONLY*, IT SEEMS, TO FIND HIS SUBJECTS BECOME *ASSASSINS!*

AND YET, T'CHALLA --IF THEY THOUGHT WE WERE *INTRUDERS*--!

NO MATTER!

W'KABI--SPEAK THE *COMMAND* I GAVE BEFORE I DEPARTED THIS LAND!

WE...WERE *NEVER* TO USE OUR WEAPONS AGAINST *MEN*...EXCEPT BY *ROYAL ORDER!*

BUT, MIGHTY *CHIEFTAIN*--

THAT ORDER HAS BEEN *GIVEN!*

...BY HIM WHO *RULES* FOR YOU--BY *M'BAKU!*

5

I HAVE LONG *AWAITED* THIS HALCYON HOMECOMING, MIGHTY CHIEFTAIN!

THOUGH YOURS IS THE SACRED *PANTHER POWER*--THOUGH NONE IN THE JUNGLE HAS EVER MATCHED YOUR *PROWESS*--

STILL, ONLY *ONE* MAY SIT THE THRONE OF WAKANDA!

AND, THAT *ONE* MUST EVER BE... *M'BAKU!*

YET, EVEN A *VILLAIN* MAY SMILE...AND SMILE...

WELCOME, ONCE AND EVER CHIEFTAIN, TO YOUR *HOMELAND!*

COMMANDS WHICH WE MUST *DISCUSS*, OLD FRIEND! AFTER THE *BLACK KNIGHT* AND MY FELLOW *AVENGERS* ARE SEEN TO!

A THOUSAND *PARDONS* FOR THE GUN-CRAZED FOOLS WHO MISCONSTRUED MY *COMMANDS!*

OF *COURSE,* O T'CHALLA!

THIS IS INDEED A DAY FOR *FEASTING!*

...SO YOU SEE, MY ORDERS WERE *NOT* ILL-CONSIDERED!

REPORTS HAVE COME TO ME THAT YOUR OLD ENEMY, *KLAW,* IS AFOOT ONCE MORE!

A SIMPLE *CALL* TO ME WOULD HAVE *DISPELLED* SUCH RUMORS, M'BAKU!

KLAW LANGUISHES IN *PRISON...*WHERE HE HAS EVER *BELONGED!*

STILL, PERHAPS YOUR *MOTIVES* WERE BETTER THAN YOUR *JUDGMENT!*

I SHALL *WITHHOLD* MY *VERDICT....!*

SO *THIS* IS T'CHALLA'S *KINGDOM*--

--WHICH HE LEFT TO SERVE THE *WHOLE* OF *HUMANITY!*

THIS IS *ONE* MEAL I COULD REALLY *ENJOY...*

IF ONLY I KNEW WHERE *NATASHA* IS!*

*WOULD HE? NOT IF HE PORED OVER *CAPTAIN MARVEL #12!* --STAN.

7

GAZE, AS YOUR SENSES RETURN TO YOU, ON YOUR GRAVEN *PANTHER-IMAGE*, RISING FROM ITS SUNKEN *SILO!*

SOON, IT WILL BE BUT BLACK *RUBBLE*--BENEATH WHICH *YOU* SHALL LIE BURIED!

AND IN ITS *PLACE*--LOOK *BEHIND* YOU, FOOL!

A GIANT, WHITE *GORILLA*--CARVED OF NEW-HEWN *STONE!*

WHAT *TREACHERY* IS THIS, M'BAKU?

CALL IT WHAT YOU *WILL!*

TO ME, THAT COLOSSUS IS A TOWERING--*SYMBOL!*

A SYMBOL THAT A *NEW* DAY HAS DAWNED IN WAKANDA--

THE DAY OF THE *MAN-APE!*

HE *MISSED* ME--AS IF ON *PURPOSE*--AND SPLINTERED THAT *TREE* BEHIND ME!

BUT, WHAT IS THE *SOURCE* OF HIS NEW-FOUND, INCREDIBLE *STRENGTH?*

NO MATTER *NOW!*

FIRST, WITH THE SPEED OF THE *BEAST* WHOSE NAME I BEAR--

THE *BLACK PANTHER* MUST *STRIKE!*

9

RISE, O CHIEF!

PROVE THE *FALSEHOOD* OF M'BAKU'S CLAIMS!

AY--SHOW US THAT YOU ARE NO MAN'S *LACKEY*--GROWN *SOFT* FROM YOUR STAYS IN *OTHER LANDS!*

THEN... *THAT* IS THE *REASON*...

THE REASON WHY I MUST FIGHT THIS TRAITOR... *ALONE!*

SERVILE, WHIMPERING *SCUM!*

HAS NOT M'BAKU DECREED THAT *NONE* SHOULD SPEAK TO HIM WHO IS *CHALLENGED?*

NO-- *NO!!*

NOW, YOU SHALL SPEAK TO *NO ONE*--

NOT UNTIL THE BATTLE IS LONG SINCE *DECIDED!*

SO--I *AM* CHALLENGED... BY ANCIENT *TRIBAL LAW!*

THEN, LET THE--

HOLD! THAT SLIGHT *RUSTLING* BEHIND ME--!

AIIEEEE! MERCY!!

THEY ALWAYS CRY *FIRST* TO RECEIVE MERCY--

WHO WOULD BE THE *LAST* TO BESTOW IT,!!

THWOP

11

SUCH GOLDEN WORDS MAY SERVE YOU WELL IN THE *OUTER* WORLD, PUNY ONE!

BUT, IN THE *JUNGLE,* THEY ONLY WASTE PRECIOUS *MOMENTS*--

DURING WHICH I CAN TURN THIS UPROOTED *TREE*--INTO A DEADLY *MISSILE!*

AND SO IT *WOULD* HAVE BEEN--BUT FOR MY *PANTHER SPEED!*

BUT, I CANNOT PROVE MY CAUSE BY MERE *FLIGHT!*

MUST GAIN TIME TO *THINK* --TO PLOT A *STRATEGY!*

THERE-- IN THE DARKENED *CONTROL CENTER* OF MY MAN-MADE JUNGLE!

STOP, M'BAKU!

THINK OF WHAT YOU ARE DOING TO YOUR FELLOW *TRIBES-MEN*--TO *YOURSELF!*

WOULD YOU *WIPE OUT* ALL PROGRESS --TURN THE WAKANDAS BACK DOWN THE ROAD TO *SAVAGERY?*

AY, PANTHER--

FOR, ONLY IN A *PRIMITIVE* WORLD IS *POWER* ITS OWN REWARD!

IT IS *USELESS* TO TRADE WORDS WITH THAT HUMAN BEHEMOTH!

BUT, AT LEAST I HAVE LED HIM AWAY FROM THE CAPTIVE *AVENGERS,* AND--

WAIT!

IT IS *BEYOND BELIEF!* HE *SMASHED* DOWN THE DOOR WITH ONE BLOW!

YOU MIGHT AS WELL TAKE REFUGE IN A HUT OF *STRAW,* JACKAL--

--AS HOPE THAT MERE *METAL* COULD SHIELD YOU FROM M'BAKU!

12

YOUR DEFEAT WAS SCRAWLED IN THE *WIND,* FOOL!

IF MERE *HERBS* GAVE YOU THE SKILLS OF THE STALKING *PANTHER...*

HOW MUCH GREATER IS MY *BRUTE STRENGTH--* STRENGTH OBTAINED FROM THE FLESH AND BLOOD OF THE FABLED *WHITE GORILLA!!*

STEP INTO THE *LIGHT--* AND *END* THIS FARCE!

THUS SHALL IT END, *TRAITOR--* WITH YOUR TOTAL *DEFEAT--* AND *DISGRACE!*

--AARRGHHH!--

HE SPRAWLS STILL AS *DEATH* ITSELF!

COULD ONE STEALTHY *BLOW--* STRUCK IN *DARKNESS--* HAVE DOWNED HIM?

IT WOULD SEEM *NOT,* AND YET--

HERE HE LIES --SILENT, UNMOVING--

VICTORY, IT WOULD SEEM, IS *MINE!*

BUT THERE IS NO JOY IN THE FALL OF HIM I ONCE *TRUSTED--*

--HIM I ONCE CALLED... *FRIEND!*

13

HE SLAMMED THE DYNAMO *DOWNWARD* --AT *HURRICANE* SPEED!

THE *FORCE* ALONE WOULD HAVE BEEN *FATAL*--

UNLESS IT BE IN THE CLAMMY *QUIET* OF THE *GRAVE*!!

T*HOOM!*

--TO ONE NOT ENDOWED WITH *CATLIKE* PROWESS--

INCLUDING THE ABILITY TO LAND ALWAYS ON ONE'S SUPPLE *LIMBS*!

BUT, IT *ALSO* MATTERS *WHERE* ONE LANDS, PANTHER!

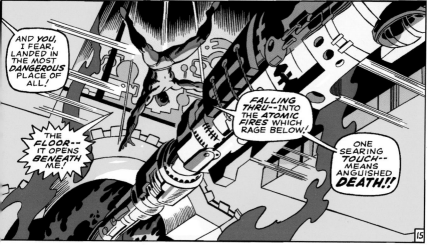

AND *YOU*, I FEAR, LANDED IN THE MOST *DANGEROUS* PLACE OF *ALL*!

THE *FLOOR*-- IT OPENS *BENEATH* ME!

FALLING *THRU*--INTO THE *ATOMIC FIRES* WHICH RAGE BELOW!

ONE SEARING *TOUCH*-- MEANS ANGUISHED *DEATH*!!

15

BROKE MY FALL-- MERE **INCHES** FROM A FIERY END!

YET, EVEN ONE INCH IS FAR ENOUGH--

--IF IT LEAVES THE BLACK PANTHER ALIVE TO **FIGHT**-- TO **ENDURE**--TO CONQUER!

BUT, WHICH **WAY** LIES THE PATH TO SAFETY?

AHEAD ROARS THE ATOMIC **FURNACE**-- MOLTEN, SEETHING!

WHILE, **BEHIND** ME--

--WAITS **DOOM!!**

M'BAKU!

I SHOULD HAVE KNOWN YOU WOULD NEVER TRUST THE **NUCLEAR FLAMES** TO DO YOUR HANDI- WORK!

IT **PLEASES** ME THAT YOU WERE SPARED THAT FORM OF DEATH, HAPLESS ONE--

--THAT I **MYSELF** MIGHT-- YEEOWWWR!

YOU NEED NOT **FINISH** YOUR SNARLING THREATS, MAN-APE...

THE *BLACK PANTHER* HAS HEARD SUCH DIRE MOUTHINGS *BEFORE*-- AS HE HAS FOUGHT ALONGSIDE THE *FANTASTIC FOUR*-- CAPTAIN *AMERICA*-- THE MIGHTY *AVENGERS!*

--*UHHNNN!*

MUST *DESTROY* YOU --*MUST*--!

WAIT! YOU'RE FALL-ING--!

YOUR DAYS OF DESTRUCTION --OF TYRANNY-- ARE *ENDED!* NOW--

GOT YOU!

SAVE ME, T'CHALLA --*SAVE* ME!

I WAS A *FOOL* --TO USURP YOUR THRONE!

PULL ME UP!!

NO MATTER WHAT YOUR *DESERTS,* M'BAKU... I *SHALL* SAVE YOU... IN THE NAME OF *PERISHED FRIEND-SHIP!*

YES--YES-- AND I SHALL FAITH-FULLY *SERVE* YOU ONCE AGAIN--

BUT HURRY-- *HURRY!*

AY, HURRY... THAT ALL THE SOONER I MAY *TASTE*--

SKRUNCH

17

VICTORY!!

ZAKKAZAK

OHHH!

I--EXPECTED TREACHERY-- BUT DID NOT GUESS ITS SOURCE!

CAN'T STAND-- THE SHOCK!- BLACK- ING OUT!

OH NO, MY DEAR CHIEFTAIN!

YOU SHALL NOT PLUMMET HEADLONG INTO INSTANT OBLIVION!

OTHERS MUST WITNESS YOUR DESTRUCTION-- AND TREMBLE...

THAT NEVER- MORE SHALL ANY DARE TO CHALLENGE... M'BAKU THE MAN-APE!

THUS, WHEN T'CHALLA'S CATLIKE EYES ONCE MORE PIERCE THE GLOOM, THEY BEHOLD--

YOUR VAUNTED PANTHER-IMAGE... DECADENT SYMBOL OF YOUR WEAK- KNEED RULE!

SOON IT WILL TOPPLE UPON YOU...AND WITH ITS FALL...

DARKNESS RETURNS AGAIN TO THE PRIMEVAL JUNGLE!

PROVING NOTHING, MY FRIEND...

...EXCEPT THAT YOU ARE WORSE THAN A SAVAGE... YOU ARE A MADMAN!!

MAD, AM I?

COULD ANY MERE MADMAN DO THIS?

HE STRIKES THE BASE OF THE STATUE-- WITH HIS FULL, INFIDEL POWER!

HOW LONG-- BEFORE IT FALLS FORWARD --CRUSHES ME TO A PULP?

18

AT THAT VERY MOMENT, NOT FAR AWAY, *OTHERS* ARE ALSO AWAKENING...REMEMBERING A GLOATING *HOST*, AND A SIP OF TAINTED *WINE*...

THAT CRUMB *M'BAKU*--HE MUST HAVE *DOUBLE-CROSSED* THE PANTHER!

BUT, WHAT CAN WE DO--STRIPPED OF OUR *WEAPONS*!

YOU TWO MAY HAVE BEEN *ROBBED* OF ARROWS AND SWORD!

BUT, *NO MAN* MAY DEPRIVE THE *VISION* OF--

THE POWER OF A MASSIVE *BATTERING RAM*!!

KRAAK!

NOW, HURRY-- EACH SECOND MAY BE *VITAL*--!

MMFFF!

WHAT *INSANITY* IS THIS?

THE PANTHER STATUE *TILTS*...

BUT DOES NOT *TOPPLE!*

IT *MUST* FALL--*IT MUST!*

FOR, IN M'BAKU'S VEINS NOW FLOWS THE BLOOD OF THE UNHOLY *WHITE GORILLA!*

THE BLACK PANTHER MUST *DIE*-- THAT THE DAY OF THE *MAN-APE* MAY BEGIN!

THE STATUE MUST FALL!!

WAIT!

THAT RUMBLING, CRACKING *NOISE!*

THE IDOL ISN'T *FALLING*-- IT'S *CRUMBLING*--

CRUMBLING--

19